Princess Bea's
Pony Parade

PRINCESS POWER

Princess Bea's
Pony Parade

Sudipta Bardhan-Quallen

AMULET BOOKS • NEW YORK

Cataloging-in-Publication Data has been applied for and may be obtained from the Library of Congress.

ISBN 978-1-4197-7203-0

PRINCESS POWER™/© Netflix. Used with permission.
Based on *Princesses Wear Pants* created by Savannah Guthrie
and Allison Oppenheim
Interior illustrations by Thais Bolton
Book design by Brann Garvey and Becky James

Published in 2024 by Amulet Books, an imprint of ABRAMS.

Printed and bound in the U.S.A.
10 9 8 7 6 5 4 3 2 1

Amulet Books are available at special discounts when purchased in quantity for premiums and promotions as well as fundraising or educational use. Special editions can also be created to specification. For details, contact specialsales@abramsbooks.com or the address below.

Amulet Books® is a registered trademark of Harry N. Abrams, Inc.

ABRAMS The Art of Books
195 Broadway, New York, NY 10007
abramsbooks.com

To the Smithies of Parsons House—
you've got the power!
—S.B.Q.

Meet the princesses

Bea Blueberry

An athlete who's usually up for a challenge, Bea loves extreme sports and jumping into action.

Kira Kiwi

An animal expert with a caring heart, Kira has never met a creature she didn't love.

of the Four Fruitdoms!

Rita Raspberry

As the resident artist of the Four Fruitdoms, Rita always brings some razzle-dazzle to every situation.

Penny Pineapple

With her curious mind and her love of science, Penny can solve big problems in a pinch.

Chapter 1

Princess Bea of the Blueberry Fruitdom knew she had one very important responsibility—to help her fruitizens with anything they needed. She took that responsibility very, *very* seriously.

Today, the fruitizens who needed her help were Bea's fathers, King Barton and Sir Benedict.

Bea raced through the palace, looking for her fathers. She found them tucked under the blankets. "Hi, Pop! Hi, Dad!" Bea called to King Barton and Sir Benedict. "Are you both ready for the Hullabaloo?"

The Horse and Harvest Hullabaloo was an annual Blueberry Fruitdom tradition. Right after the first blueberry harvest of the year, Bernie, the royal stallion, led a parade all through the fruitdom. Pop and Dad usually took turns riding him, but Bernie was always the star. Bea got the really fun job—giving out bushels of blueberries to cheering fruitizens.

This year, Bea and her friend Princess Penny Pineapple had something new planned. Instead of just handing out blueberry bushels, Penny used her science skills to build a Blueberry Blaster. It could launch a bunch of blueberry bushels at the same time. That meant fruitizens could get their fresh berries even more quickly!

"No, we are not ready!" Pop moaned.

Dad groaned, "We might have to cancel the Hullabaloo."

"I think Benedict gave me the flu," Pop answered, wiping his nose with a tissue.

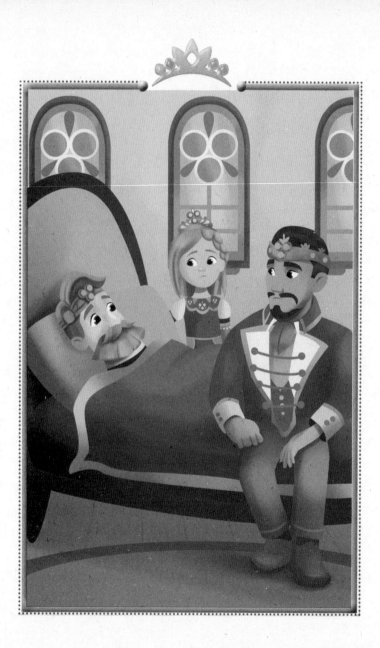

"Who?" Dad asked, frowning. "Who gave *who* the flu? I think I got it from you!"

"Ugh!" Bea cried. "Don't rhyme!"

"True," Pop said, shaking his head. "Rhyming makes our daughter blue. And it doesn't help anyone get over the flu. The important thing is the Hullabaloo. What will we do?"

Bea rolled her eyes, even though she was smiling. "First, you're both going to stop rhyming. Why are dads so un-funny?"

"That's not true!" Dad said.

Dad started to cough, so Pop added, "We're funny as . . . *achoo*!" He winked at Dad. "We rhymed again!"

Bea couldn't help it. She giggled out loud at that last joke. But then she got serious. She waited for her fathers to stop grinning and said, "We can't cancel the Hullabaloo. Everyone is so excited for it!"

"But I can't ride through the fruitdom like this!" Dad exclaimed. He loudly blew his nose.

"Neither can I," Pop said. "It's too bad. I know Bernie was looking forward to his day to shine."

Bea thought for a moment. They were right. Neither of her fathers could lead a parade with the flu. She could still go hand out the blueberry bushels. But then who would ride Bernie?

Suddenly, Bea had an idea. "Bernie can still lead the parade!" she announced. "I'll ride him. I'll get Kira, Penny, and Rita to help me hand out blueberry bushels while you two get some rest. The Hullabaloo is still a go!"

Chapter 2

Are you sure, Bea?" Pop asked. "You've never ridden Bernie before."

"In fact, I don't think I've ever seen you on any of the royal horses," Dad said.

"No, but riding can't be harder than hang gliding or zip-lining," Bea said, shrugging. "All I have to do is learn to ride a horse by tomorrow and lead the parade? Challenge accepted!"

Bea's fathers glanced at each other. Then they nodded. "If you're sure, Bea," Dad said. "We trust you."

"Just don't be afraid to ask for help," Pop added.

"Score!" Bea exclaimed. She rushed toward the door, shouting, "This is going to be epic!"

Bea shouted a quick good-bye to her fathers and rushed to the Royal Stables. On the way, she heard a BOOM. The

noise was coming from the Pineapple Fruitdom. *That must be Penny testing the Blueberry Blaster,* she thought. *It's loud!*

Before Bea could think about how much boom was too much boom, she arrived at the Royal Stables. As the royal stallion, Bernie had the biggest stall in a quiet corner of the building. Bea spied him snacking on some oats. He looked happy and strong. *And big!* she thought. *I never noticed that before.*

Bea knew Bernie was taller than she was. He was even taller than either of her fathers. But up close, Bernie was as tall as two of Bea. When he stomped a hoof, Bea thought she felt the ground shaking.

As she stepped toward Bernie, Bea felt nervous and sweaty. It wasn't her favorite way to sweat!

Bernie looked right at Bea and snorted. "Eeek!" Bea shrieked. She backed away.

Bernie snorted again. He pawed at the ground with his front hoof.

Bea wasn't sure why Bernie seemed so scary to her. She just knew she was scared! She spun around and raced away.

When Bea reached the stable door, she slumped against it. "What was I thinking?" she whispered to herself. Horses weren't like hang gliders or zip lines—they were huge and terrifying and had minds of their own!

Unfortunately, Bea had made a promise that Bernie would lead the Hullabaloo. *I have to keep my word*, she thought. *So I have to figure out some way to make that happen.*

Standing up tall, Bea brushed the hay off her clothes. She put her hands on her hips. "I'll have nothing to show for it if I don't go for it!" she declared. She decided she'd go for it, but there was no way she could do it by herself. "I need to use Princess Power for this!"

Chapter 3

Bea touched the blueberry-shaped charm on her friendship bracelet. It hummed and started to glow. Then a large blueberry shape bloomed in the sky! "The charm alarm will let my friends know that I need their help!" she said.

Bea poked her head inside the stable. "I'm off to the Punchbowl Treehouse, Bernie," she shouted. Bernie snorted. "I guess that's how horses say good-bye!" Bea said, laughing. "I'll be back soon!"

Bea hopped onto her hang glider and began the journey to the treehouse. When Punchbowl Island was in sight, she released the glider and grabbed the zip line. She whizzed along quickly and was standing in the treehouse in no time.

A sparkle near the shore of the Raspberry Fruitdom caught Bea's eye. It was Princess Rita in her bedazzled

sailboat. Bea also spied Princess Kira and her hamster, Mr. Scrumples, in Kira's motorboat. Both boats raced toward Punchbowl Island.

Bea heard the whirr of a plane's engine. She looked in the direction of the Pineapple Fruitdom and saw Princess Penny and her cat, Fussy, in her plane. Before she knew it, Penny and Fussy had parachuted down to the slide and were whooshing toward the treehouse.

Soon, all four friends were together, smiling and high-fiving.

"Why did you activate your charm alarm, Bea?" Rita asked.

Bea opened her mouth to tell the other princesses about her problem, but no sounds came out. *This is so embarrassing*, she thought. *I can't believe I'm scared of a horse!*

"Is there a problem in the Blueberry Fruitdom?" Kira asked.

"I need your help," Bea began. "It's almost time for the Horse and Harvest Hullabaloo."

"I love the Hullabaloo!" Penny exclaimed.

"It's the most tiara-tastic Hullabaloo of the year," Rita agreed.

"My dads are both sick," Bea continued, "so I volunteered to lead the parade. With Bernie."

"You're going to ride Bernie?" Penny asked. Her eyes grew wide. "I've never seen you ride a horse before!"

"Bicycles, Jet Skis, snowmobiles, yes," Kira said, "but no horses!"

Bea smiled weakly. "Well, this would be my first time riding," she said.

Now was the time for Bea to tell her friends that she was scared. But before she could admit that, Rita said, "You're so brave about everything! Horseback riding should be as easy for you as bedazzling is for me."

Bea gulped. Her friends were all smiling at her. She thought, *How can I tell them I'm not as brave as they think?*

Chapter 4

*B*ea decided that maybe she could wait to admit her fears to her friends. "Since the rest of the Blueberry royal family aren't healthy enough to go to the Hullabaloo, would you all help me make sure everything goes smoothly?" she asked. "And that Bernie gets to lead the parade?"

"Of course we will!" Kira said.

"We'll do whatever you need us to do," Rita said. "You know when we work together, we can do anything!"

"There's just one thing," Penny said.

The other girls frowned at Penny. "What thing?" Bea asked.

"You three can go straight back to the Blueberry Fruitdom," Penny answered.

"You know this is a high-stakes situation, right, Penny?" Rita added. "We need everyone's help!"

Penny grinned. "I know," she said.

"And I wouldn't miss helping Bea for anything. I just have to go home first. I have to bring the Blueberry Blaster to the Blueberry Palace!"

"Whoa!" Bea exclaimed. "You had me worried for a minute!"

Everyone laughed.

"You know you can always count on me," Penny said.

Bea nodded. Then she said, "There's only one thing left to do! Pinkie-tea promise!" She held out her pinkie. "We pinkie-tea promise to help those in need."

Rita, Kira, and Penny added their pinkies. "With our Princess Power we'll always succeed!" they said together.

With their pinkies extended, they all took a sip of their tea. The pinkie-tea promise was complete!

The girls got back to the Blueberry Fruitdom lightning fast. Bea knew she'd have to tell the other princesses she was too frightened to ride Bernie. *But maybe I can wait a bit longer,* she thought. *What if it isn't so scary now that I have my friends with me?*

Bernie spied the princesses and neighed. "He's excited to see us!" Kira said, laughing. She went to the stall door and reached in to pat the horse's muzzle. "Hi, Bernie," she cooed.

Rita examined Bernie's mane. "You've got some tangles, huh?" she said, smiling. "Don't worry, I'll take care of those."

Kira went into Bernie's stall. She held her hand out for Bernie to sniff. She gently stroked his mane. Bernie snorted once, but then he quieted down. Kira slipped a bridle over Bernie's head, and Rita placed a saddle on his back. Kira fastened the buckles. Then they looked at Bea. "Bernie is all ready for you," Kira said.

"Hop on!" Rita added.

Bea stood frozen a few feet away from Bernie. She couldn't make her feet step closer. *I don't know what to do*, she thought, *but I can't get on that horse!*

Chapter 5

Bernie seemed just as frightening as he was before. In fact, the stallion looked like he had grown a foot taller since this morning!

"I can't get on Bernie yet," Bea finally answered. "I just realized that I forgot my helmet. I should go back to my room and get it."

"Actually—" Kira began. But Bea didn't wait. She rushed away. Soon, she found herself slumping against the stable door again. It didn't matter that Rita and Kira had been there. She was still afraid of Bernie.

Princess Bea Blueberry was not used to being afraid. She was usually ready for any adventure. This time was different, though. And she didn't know what to do about it.

Before she had a chance to think of a solution, Bea spotted something in the sky. It was Penny's plane! There was a box attached to the grappling hook.

As the plane flew above the stables, the box was released. It floated down on its own parachute. A moment later, Penny and Fussy parachuted out, too.

"We brought the Blueberry Blaster!" Penny exclaimed.

Bea frowned. "That's a box," she said.

Penny giggled. "The Blaster is inside. Or, the pieces are. It just needs a little assembly." She started pulling things out. "I designed the Blaster with wheels to make it easy for us to move it."

Rita and Kira appeared at the stable door, interrupting Penny. "We found riding helmets inside the stable," Rita cried.

"So you can ride Bernie now," Kira added.

Bea started to feel sweaty again. The Hullabaloo was Bernie's chance to shine. It wasn't fair that *her* fear was going to ruin Bernie's big moment!

One of the wheels from Penny's box rolled away. Fussy stopped it with a paw. Suddenly, Bea thought of something. She didn't have to *ride* Bernie for the stallion to lead the parade!

"Actually," Bea said, "I have a different idea for something a lot more epic. We can use Princess Power to build an automated horse transport vehicle!"

enny, Kira, and Rita stared at Bea. Bea was grinning. Her friends were not.

"I don't understand," Rita said. "You want to build a machine that will move Bernie along the parade route?"

"Horses can move pretty well on their hooves, you know," Penny said.

"And a horse transport vehicle would have to be driven," Kira said.

"I can drive it!" Bea exclaimed.

Kira shook her head. "If you were driving, you'd be *in front* of Bernie. That would mean Bernie wasn't leading the parade."

Bea's shoulders slumped. Kira was right. Her epic idea wasn't all that epic.

"Bea," Rita said, touching Bea's arm, "is there something you want to tell us?"

Bea couldn't hold it in any longer. She sighed. "I *do* have to tell you guys something. I can't ride Bernie. I'm just too scared."

At first, Bea's friends didn't say anything. They were too shocked! Then Penny cried, "But you're never afraid of anything!"

Bea's face felt warm. She looked down at the ground so her friends wouldn't see.

Penny could tell she'd said the wrong thing. She stepped closer and put her arm around Bea's shoulder. "What I meant," she said softly, "is that I'm sorry I didn't notice you might be afraid."

"I was doing my best to hide it," Bea mumbled.

"Oh, Bea," Rita said. "You didn't have to hide that from us."

"We're your friends," Kira added. "You never have to hide anything."

Bea sniffled. "I know that. I don't know why I didn't just say something."

"It's all right," Rita said. "No one likes to admit that they're scared." She squeezed Bea's hand.

"We can help you with Bernie," Kira said. "I know about horses. I can teach you how to ride."

"We'll actually do anything you need us to do," Rita added.

Bea nodded. "Thank you," she said softly.

"I'm going to bring Bernie out to this pen," Kira said, pointing.

"I'll grab one of those riding helmets," Rita said.

"And I'll finish putting the Blueberry Blaster together," Penny said.

"And I'll just wait here!" Bea announced, giggling. She felt better already. She thought, *Maybe Princess Power will get me past my fear!*

Chapter 7

Kira stroked Bernie's nose as she led him out. Rita followed behind, carrying a riding helmet. "Here you go, Bea," she said.

Bea examined the helmet. There was a tiara attached to it! "Was this helmet always so sparkly?" she asked.

Rita shrugged. "I *may* have had enough time to spruce it up," she said, smiling. "Besides, a tiara goes with everything!"

"Bernie is ready for you, Bea," Kira called.

Bea put the helmet on and walked into the pen. The stallion was being very gentle with Kira. *I can do this*, Bea thought.

"Let's get you into the saddle, Bea," Kira said. "Put your foot in the stirrup there. Then swing your other leg over Bernie's back."

Bea gulped. But she didn't move. And she couldn't explain why! Finally, she asked, "Can I just watch someone else first?"

"Of course," Kira replied. "Rita or Penny, which one of you wants to ride Bernie?"

"I'll volunteer!" Rita said. She took the riding helmet from Bea. "I wanted to try the tiara helmet anyway." She climbed into the saddle.

"When you're sitting on a horse," Kira explained to Bea, "it's important to get comfortable and relax."

Bea nodded.

"Make sure you feel balanced before you try to get moving," Kira said.

"Like you balance on a dirt bike?" Bea asked.

"Exactly!" Kira said. "Except you won't need to pedal on Bernie. And he won't tip over as easily as a bike."

"Score!" Bea exclaimed.

"Always hold on to the reins," Kira continued. "They're your brakes and your steering."

"So the reins are like the handlebars?" Bea asked.

Kira nodded. "To start moving, click your tongue. That tells Bernie to go."

Rita clicked. Bernie began to walk.

"If you want to go faster, make a kissing sound," Kira added. "But it's OK to keep it slow for now."

"Thank sequins!" Rita cried.

"Gently tug on the left rein if you want Bernie to go left," Kira said.

"And if I wanted to go right, I'd tug on the right rein?" Bea asked.

Kira nodded. "Yes!"

Rita rode Bernie all the way around the pen. When they got back to Kira, Rita jumped out of the saddle.

"Well, Bea?" Kira asked. "Are you ready to try to ride now?"

Bea squared her shoulders. She saw her friends smiling at her, and she wanted to get up in that saddle more than anything. She stepped closer and almost put her foot in the stirrup.

Then, there was a loud BOOM! Bernie neighed and reared up on his hind legs. Bea shrieked.

"Fussy!" Penny shouted. "What did you do?"

Fussy had decided to take a nap on the control panel of the Blueberry Blaster. Unfortunately, her paw hit the launch button by accident. An empty bushel got blasted into the air. The sound scared Bernie. And then Bernie scared Bea!

Bea's heart thumped in her chest. Even though Kira calmed Bernie down, Bea made a decision. "I'm really sorry," she said, gulping. "I still can't do it. I can't ride Bernie. I'm too scared!"

Chapter 8

S tink bug!" Penny cried. She lifted
Fussy off of the control panel and
plopped her onto the ground. "That is
not a cat bed!"

Fussy meowed and then curled up to nap in the shade.

"I'm really sorry about that," Penny said. "The Blaster is louder than I thought."

"Loud noises can upset horses," Kira explained. "But Bernie is feeling better now."

That didn't matter to Bea. She covered her face with her hands. She didn't want anyone to see her crying.

Rita came over and stood near Bea. "Hey," she said softly, "it's OK. You do *not* have to ride Bernie at all."

"Rita is right," Penny said. "You don't have to do anything you don't want to do."

"And it's all right to feel scared of something," Kira added. "In fact, it's all right to be afraid of anything at all!" She smiled. "I'm afraid of zombies."

Bea sniffled. "Zombies aren't real," she mumbled.

"They're still terrifying!" Penny said. "Don't laugh, but I'm scared of peanut butter sticking to the roof of my mouth."

"And I'm scared of running out of glitter," Rita said. When everyone laughed, Rita frowned. "It's a serious fear!"

"We know, Rita," Kira soothed, patting her friend's shoulder.

Bea wiped her eyes. "What am I going to do now? The Hullabaloo is tomorrow."

Bea's friends looked at each other. Then Penny said, "Every princess problem has a princess solution."

"And the solution here might be," Kira added, "that you guide Bernie through the parade route with a lead rope."

Bea shook her head. "Then *Bernie* wouldn't be leading the parade," she answered.

"Bernie could pull you in a wagon," Penny said. "That way he'd be in front."

"I wanted this to be the most epic Hullabaloo ever," Bea said, frowning. "Riding a horse is epic. Riding in a wagon is the opposite of epic."

"Well," Rita said, "one of us could ride Bernie for you."

"But a Blueberry Royal is supposed to ride in the Hullabaloo," Bea wailed.

"We know," Penny said. "But at least there still would *be* a parade."

"Can't I just let Bernie go first?" Bea asked. "He knows the way. I can walk behind him."

Kira shook her head. "You've seen how horses can get startled by unexpected things," she said. "With the crowd at the Hullabaloo, anything could happen. Someone could scream, or throw something, or run across the road in front of Bernie. Without someone controlling the horse, other people could get hurt."

Bea frowned harder. There was no good princess solution to this problem.

"You can decide tomorrow morning," Rita suggested. "We'll be back in the morning to help you set up the parade."

"And with the Blueberry Blaster," Penny added.

"And with Bernie," Kira finished.

Bea sighed. "See you tomorrow, I guess." What else could she do?

The morning of the Hullabaloo, Bea woke up early. She'd been tossing and turning all night. She still wasn't excited about any of the plans her friends had suggested. *If I could have just been brave*, she thought, *this would be the amazing Hullabaloo I wanted!* She was fine with so many sports—skateboarding, water-skiing, hang gliding. She never imagined horseback riding would be the *one* sport that was too extreme for Princess Bea Blueberry.

All of a sudden, Bea had an idea. "Why didn't I think of this yesterday?" she cried. She grabbed her skateboard and spun the wheels. *Just like the wheels on the Blaster*, she thought.

Bea rushed out to the stables. "Hi, Bernie! Are you ready for Plan Bea?" She held up her skateboard.

Bernie neighed and tossed his head. He looked confused.

Bea rummaged through the stable supplies. "I need your saddle and two lead ropes." She placed the saddle on a rack. Then she tied one rope to each side. She moved her skateboard behind the saddle.

Just then, the other princesses arrived. "Hi, Bea!" Rita called. "We're here!"

"What did you decide on for the parade?" Kira asked.

"Lead rope, wagon, or Kira?" Penny added.

"None of those!" Bea answered.

The girls frowned. "You're not cancel-ing the Hullabaloo, are you?" Rita asked.

"No way," Bea replied. "I just came up with the princess solution we didn't think of yesterday!" She pointed to her arrangement of ropes and skateboard. "Have you ever heard of horse-skate-surfing?"

Her friends all opened their mouths. But no one said anything!

"Of course you haven't," Bea said. "I just invented it!" She explained her plan. "Bernie knows the parade route, so he can go first. He'll pull me behind him on my skateboard. I'll hold on with some ropes."

"It's a good idea," Penny said, "but it

needs a few modifications." She took out her science kit. "If you're going to surf behind Bernie," she said, "he needs a different harness. Something that will make it easier for him to pull your weight." She sketched something in her lab notebook. "If my calculations are correct, it should look like this."

"Can you make me one of those?" Bea asked.

"Does Rita bedazzle in her sleep?" Penny answered, grinning.

"I do!" Rita exclaimed.

Kira looked over Penny's plans. "We should add a harness pad under this part," she said, pointing. "That'll be more comfortable for Bernie."

"Good thinking!" Penny said.

The girls worked together to build the new harness. Kira made sure it was put on Bernie properly. Then Bea clipped on the two ropes, one on each side of the harness.

"Science success!" Penny said.

"Sparkle success, too," Rita said. She held out something glittery. "I made this for Bernie yesterday." She slipped it over Bernie's head so it covered his ears. "Kira said loud noises can spook horses. So I made this bonnet for Bernie to wear. That way, the Blueberry Blaster won't seem as loud to him."

"Teenykin-tastic, Rita!" Kira exclaimed.

Bernie looked very handsome in his new bonnet. He nodded his head at Bea like he was saying, *Come on already!*

But Bea *still* wasn't ready! She turned around and shouted, "I just need another minute!"

Chapter 10

Uh, Bea," Kira called, "we don't have a lot of time. The parade needs to start now!"

"I know!" Bea replied. She picked a

riding helmet and strapped it on. "Safety first!"

The other princesses sighed in relief.

Bea placed her skateboard behind Bernie. She grabbed the ropes and stepped on the skateboard. "Ready, Bernie?" Bea asked.

The stallion pawed the ground with his front leg.

"That means he's ready," Kira said.

"Let's go!" Bea cried. She clicked her tongue like Kira showed her.

Bernie took a few steps forward. Bea was pulled along on her skateboard. "Now, a little faster," Bea said. She made a kissing sound to make Bernie speed up.

The stallion moved faster. Bea held on more tightly to the ropes. She shifted around so she was balanced on the skateboard. Soon, Bernie was galloping—and Bea was racing behind!

It was a little like waterskiing, but instead of a motorboat on the water pulling her on water skis, Bea was using a horse to pull her on a skateboard on the ground. "Whoa!" Bea shouted. "This is amazing!"

"If you're done practicing," Kira said, "you'd better get to the front of the parade!"

"You don't want them to start without you!" Rita added.

The only Blueberry fruitizens who hadn't lined up to watch the Hullabaloo were King Barton and Sir Benedict. They waved from the palace balcony, with blankets wrapped around their bodies. Then they went back to resting so they could get better soon.

The crowd let out a cheer when Bea led Bernie to the front of the parade. "Are you ready, buddy?" Bea asked.

Bernie neighed and nodded his head.

Bea set up her skateboard behind Bernie again. The horse-skate-surfing began! Bernie knew exactly where to go. Bea just made sure she hung on tight and rolled with the curves!

"What is Princess Bea doing?" someone in the crowd asked.

"I don't know," someone else answered, "but I want to try!"

Bea grinned. As much fun as it was to horse-skate-surf, it was even better to know her fruitizens thought it was a cool idea!

Kira and Rita pulled the Blueberry Blaster behind Bea and Bernie. Penny used her controller to aim and launch the bushels of blueberries into the crowd. She'd also added a cat-bed shelf to make sure there were no more accidental launches! Rita's bonnet worked really well—Bernie didn't get startled by the blasting sound at all!

Bernie enjoyed every moment of his time as the star. He held his head up high and neighed at the crowd. He even stopped every once in a while to pose for pictures!

When Bernie trotted up to the door of the Royal Stables, Bea couldn't believe how quickly the parade had come to an end.

"You did it, Bea!" Rita cried. "The most sparkle-acious, awesome Hullabaloo ever!"

"And you invented a new sport!" Penny added.

"Most importantly," Kira said, "you made sure Bernie got his special moment in a teenykin-tastic parade!"

"I couldn't have done it without you all," Bea replied. She pulled her friends into a big group hug. "Princess teamwork for the win!"

Even if a fear feels weird, it's probably more common than you think! Doctors call Bea's fear of horses *equinophobia*. Kira's fear of zombies is called *kinemortophobia*. Penny's fear of peanut butter sticking to the roof of your mouth is *arachibutyrophobia*. *Sparkalaphobia* is the irrational fear of glittery or sparkly things, which is the opposite of Rita's fear—but that probably has a name, too!

Read more fruit-tastic adventures . . .

. . . and don't miss:

Now on Netflix!

About the Author

Sudipta Bardhan-Quallen is an award-winning author whose work includes *Roxie Loves Adventure*, *Tyrannosaurus Wrecks!*, the Purrmaids chapter book series, and more than sixty other books. A princess at heart, she enjoys dressing up and being pampered—but she's always up for tackling problems and getting her hands dirty. Sudipta lives in New Jersey with her husband, three kids, and an adorable pug named Roxie. Find out more about her and her books by visiting sudipta.com.